Destiny's BIG IDEA

Look for these and other books about Linelle Destiny in the Linelle Destiny Series:

Visit www.thesecretsistersclub.com

Linelle Destiny Series

Destiny's BIG IDEA

Dr. Alicia Holland

Illustrations by Anoop PC

This book may be ordered through booksellers or by contacting:

iGlobal Educational Services, LLC
PO Box 7404
Round Rock, Texas 78683-7404
www.iglobaleducation.com
512-761-5898

Because of the dynamic nature of the Internet, any web addresses or links contained in this book may have changed since publication and may no longer be valid. The views expressed in this work are solely those of the author and do not necessarily reflect the views of the publisher, and the publisher hereby disclaims any responsibility for them.

This is a work of fiction. Names, characters, businesses, places, events, and incidents are either the products of the author's imagination or used in a fictitious manner. Any resemblance to actual persons, living or dead, or actual events is purely coincidental.

Linelle Destiny Series: **Destiny's Big Idea**

ISBN-13: 978-09882271-8-7

Acknowledgements

I want to first honor God for placing in my heart to share my story with others. It was He whom brought Jessica Berdei and I together to manifest this project. I am so grateful for Jessica as she took my notes and helped write this fictitious book. There are truly no words to express my gratitude as you are truly a blessing.

I also want to thank Surendra Gupta for his creativity in formatting and designing this book series. You are amazing!

Dedication

I dedicate this book series to my beautiful and talented daughters, Georgia and Amaiya Johnson. Remember, you are valued, loved, and competent. You are worthy!

Part I:
The Big Idea

Chapter One
Big Dreams

When they made Thanksgiving break, they should have put it at a good time of year. But no, they just had to go and make their holiday during the wet, nasty weather right before winter. Kids should be able to enjoy their time off from school, not spend it staring out the window.

If I had my choice Thanksgiving break would be in the spring, when all the flowers are out and it's not too hot yet. That's a time to be thankful for, if you ask me.

But today? It's raining like crazy outside. Always is, this time of year. It's too cold to go playing in the rain and squishy mud, hunting for crawfish. That would at least make it interesting, but if I went out right now I'd just get a chill.

I've seen pictures of other places where the trees have changed to bright fall colors and there's a nice wind going, but no rain. That might be nice. In Many, Louisiana, the leaves just turn brown and fall off. They get all soggy and gross in the rain and that's that.

I'm Destiny, by the way. Linelle Destiny Sycamores, if you want to get fancy, but I'd rather you didn't.

Might as well fix my boredom before momma comes home and fixes it for me. Maybe if I clean the living room before I'm asked, I'll get a little extra allowance for the week. I sigh, standing up from my day bed in the dining room.

I start with dusting, cleaning the frames on the wooden TV stand in front of the big green couch. I've always liked these pictures. There's one of Momma and Pop on their wedding day, her dark hair all curled and glossy and her lips painted a deep red. Another is of my brother Keith, standing tall in his Air Force uniform with his deep brown eyes sparkling as he gets ready to go away on his first assignment.

There's one of me with my two brothers and sister too, but it's old. I was still a baby then, with my little dark head barely poking out of the blanket. My sister Michelle was holding me, with my brother Dino beside her, their hair both tightly braided into matching cornrows. Keith stood in the back, towering over all of us with his big shiny smile.

Michelle and Dino were twelve when I was born. They're twins, but Michelle looks more like me than she looks like Dino. She has a wide smile and a heart-shaped face just like mine, but she and I are as different as night and day.

Michelle always says that she changed my diapers, so I should listen to her. I'm going to be twelve next year, the same age she was when I was born, and if Momma has another kid I will never say anything to them about diapers.

It's lonely sometimes because I'm so much younger. I wish I had a sister my age who would be like my friends Barbara and Kendall. We could talk to each other about anything, no matter how silly. We would be able to help each other with homework and go on bike rides together and everything.

There's just me though. That's why I came up with a big idea to make everything better.

I finish dusting the top of the TV stand and move to the couch. There are always all sorts of things stuck between the couch cushions. I pull the dark green cushions off and sweep everything onto the floor with the broom, then inspect my treasures. A broken crayon, one of Michelle's house slippers, the remote control, three nickels, and a quarter. I always get to keep whatever change fell between the cracks, so I stuff those in my pocket and run to put the rest away.

The only thing left is the sweeping, which I love because it leaves my mind free to think. Tomorrow I start school again, and I've got to finish the plan for my big idea before then.

I've got most of it all planned, written in my notebook at school and safely hidden in my locker. I can see the pages if I close my eyes, especially the drawing with the name of my club written in big letters.

The Secret Sisters Club.

I have to keep the notebook at school because Momma might see it. She thinks I've gone "boy crazy," and keeps looking through everything I write. I'm not sure what she's looking for, but I'm not boy crazy. I've only had one boyfriend and he was a fool to let me go, so I'm single now.

There is one boy I like, a boy in my class. His name is Curtis and he's so smart and really cute. He's not like the other boys who run around chasing girls on the playground. He plays basketball and is just perfect.

Okay, so maybe I'm a little boy crazy.

Still, I have to keep the notebook secret, because if Momma reads about my club, she will tell Aunt Shirley. Gramma Lucy-Belle always said that Aunt Shirley couldn't hold water. I asked her once what that meant and she said that my aunt couldn't keep a secret. She was right too. If you want to tell the whole town something, tell Aunt Shirley, and make sure you tell her it's top secret!

Gramma Lucy-Belle always knew who could keep a secret and who couldn't. She said I was the best secret keeper in the whole family.

The thought of Gramma Lucy-Belle hits me in the stomach like a huge rock and I sink down onto the couch with my broom still in one hand. She only died a few weeks ago and I can still remember how she looked in that casket. She had her best church hat on and her deep brown skin had seemed almost waxy, like the freshly polished shoes my brother wore in the Air Force.

Something hard settles in my throat and I blink rapidly to keep from crying. Gramma Lucy-Belle would want me to get up and keep going, so that was exactly what I would do.

Besides, I have a club to start. Gramma Lucy-Belle always told me about the club she was in when she was young, how it was all about friendship and making the world a better place. That's what I want my club to be like. The girls in my club will promise to keep away from gossip and drama and will all have a future career doing something important.

Michelle would tell me that I'm being crazy and I need to pay attention to my own life instead, but she's never understood me. She always tells me that if I won't get something for helping people, I shouldn't bother. She says that if I keep on, I'll never have enough time and energy left for myself because no one will help me.

Most of my family thinks like that. They don't understand how important it is for me to make a difference in the world. That's why I have to keep this secret, because they won't understand that this could make everything better. One day, all the girls in the Secret Sisters Club will change the world and it will all be because of what got started in our little school.

I close my eyes and imagine the club name again, drawn on the piece of paper in my notebook.

The next page in my notebook has a poem I wrote for Mrs. Elena's class. I turn the page slowly in my mind, not really wanting to. I should work on it, though. A week after we get back from Thanksgiving break we will need to stand up in front of the class and say it from memory.

The memory won't be a problem; it's saying it in front of people. I've had a stutter since I was a little girl and when I'm nervous it comes back. Mrs. Elena said that whoever has the best poem will be published on the poetry website she found.

I know my poem is good enough to be published. I worked on it for days and it was perfect even before the Thanksgiving break started. I'm just worried that I will stutter and mess it all up.

I take a deep breath, sweeping more slowly to calm my nerves. I should practice now.

"The love I gave you was s-s-secure..."

"Destiny?" Momma says and I get so startled I nearly drop the broom. I didn't hear her unlock the front door. Droplets of water cling to her hair and jacket and the damp air that flows into the house smells like old leaves. The screen door slams behind Momma as she carries in a heavy bag of groceries and I scramble to close the second door behind her. She looks around suspiciously as she walks through the living room on her way to the kitchen. "Who are you talking to?"

"No one, Momma. I was just reciting the Pledge of Allegiance," I tell her, scooping up the dust bunnies I've collected with my broom and hoping she won't catch me in the lie.

"The pledge of allegiance? What for?"

I don't know what to say, so I just shrug as I throw away the dust.

"Well," Momma calls from the kitchen above the rustling sounds of the grocery bag. "Come wash your hands, then shell these purple hull peas for dinner. Your sister and brother will be home soon. Where's Pop?"

I point at the bedroom he and Momma share, where he's been laying pretty much all month to recover from his accident at work.

Momma nods. "Hasn't been straining his back, has he?"

"No ma'am," I answer, then rub the bar of soap between my hands. As I shell the peas, my mind goes back to the Secret Sisters Club and I smile. I can't wait for school tomorrow.

Chapter Two
Secret Sisters

I climb up the bus steps quickly, glad to be out of the cold before the drizzle turns into a serious rain. I walk back to the sixth row, where I always sit. It's the perfect spot on the bus, far enough back that most people won't push past me and my friends, but close enough to the front that the bumps don't send us flying off our seats. Plus, the old dusty smell on every bus isn't so bad here.

Curtis, the boy I like, gets on at the next stop and I look at him out of the corner of my eye. He is tall and thin, with dark brown skin and big hazel eyes. He's the dreamiest guy I've ever seen and he's nice, too. One day, I will talk to him, but not today. I have to focus on what I'm going to tell Barbara and Kendall right now. If they don't like my club idea, I don't know what I'll do.

When Barbara climbs on the bus, her skinny little body swallowed up in a giant coat, I have to stop myself from jumping

14

up and down and waving. She slumps down onto the bench seat next to me, blowing her hot breath onto her fingers to warm them.

"It's plenty cold," she complains, wrinkling her button nose as she huddles further into her oversized coat, "but it never snows! Just one snow day is all I'm asking for."

When I don't answer right away, she shoves me with one of her pointy elbows.

"Hey, are you even listening to me?"

"Sorry," I tell her, as I shake off my thoughts. "I was thinking."

"What about?"

"You gotta wait. I wanna tell you and Kendall together."

Barbara looks at me like she's going to turn my head inside out and read my mind like one of her books. "All right," she says finally, "but only if you help me keep warm."

By the time we get to Kendall's stop, my arm is falling asleep from wrapping part of my jacket around Barbara. I wave out the window at Kendall, but she has her head ducked low, her razor straight black hair falling over her face.

She walks slowly to the seat across the aisle from us, then throws herself down into her seat. When she looks up at us, her golden brown cheeks are streaked with tears.

"I dunno what to do," Kendall whispers, her narrow eyes puffed up from crying. "If the guy who owns our house really does sell..." She shakes her head, dabbing her eyes with a tissue.

"How can they sell your house without telling you?" I ask, my chest feeling hot. This isn't fair.

"Since we're renting, they can do whatever they want," Kendall shrugs sadly. "They're supposed to tell us first if they wanna sell, but they didn't"

Barbara hands Kendall another tissue. "How'd you find out?"

"My parents got told that the house has to be clean Wednesday because they are gonna show it to some guy."

Barbara and I look at each other, but we aren't sure what to say.

"Mom said," she continues, "we might not even have until Christmas to move out. We might be homeless for Christmas!" Her voice cracks suddenly and her sniffles disappear into quiet sobs into her tissue.

"You can come live at our house," I tell her, but even as I say it, I'm not sure where her family would sleep. "It'll be great," I finish lamely.

Kendall is already shaking her head, her thin lips pressed tightly together. "Dad would never agree to that," she says quietly. "He always gets really mad at the idea of taking charity from people."

"But... But people should always help each other," I say, but Barbara is already shaking her head at me.

"Not right now, Destiny." Barbara says that a lot. She says that helping other people is my soapbox and that sometimes I have to not talk about it. This time I listen to her because Kendall seems so upset.

"Please," Kendall grabs both of our hands. "Please don't tell anyone about this." She begs. "I don't wanna have a bunch of gossip about me."

✧ ✧ ✧

Barbara smiles, patting her hand awkwardly. "We're like sisters," she tells Kendall. "You can tell us anything. We won't gossip about you."

"Thanks, I'm glad to have sisters like that." Kendall smiles through her tears. "My brothers would tell everyone if I had a secret."

All three of us laugh. "My family does that too," I tell her and Barbara nods in agreement.

I suddenly remember about the club and hop up and down in excitement. "Oh, I have something to tell you two!"

"Oh, right. I completely forgot. I had to wait until you got here for her to tell us about it," Barbara tells Kendall.

"How could you forget?" I ask, my excitement suddenly paused by Barbara's loss of memory.

Barbara shrugs. "I'm super hungry. I always get distracted when I'm hungry."

"You should get something from the snack machine," Kendall tells her.

"I don't have enough. I only have a quarter."

"I have a little," I tell her, pulling the coins from the sofa out of my pocket. "I found it in the couch cushions while I was cleaning the living room."

"I have some too." Kendall scoops coins out of her pocket and we put the change together.

"All right," I tell them, "we have enough to split two snacks between the three of us."

"Chips!" Barbara exclaims.

"Cookies!" Kendall says, at the same time.

"Both!" I say and we all giggle together for a moment.

"One bag of chips, one bag of cookies," Barbara says, nodding. "Okay, so what is this big news?"

"I've been working on an idea," I tell them, wishing I had my notebook. "I want some help from you two because this is a really big idea."

Kendall grins. "Is this anything like your other big ideas?" she teases. "Remember that time you wanted to build a lemonade stand and it blew over?"

As we laugh about it, Barbara shakes her head. "The garage sale was fun, though," she says.

✧ ✧ ✧

"This is different than both of those," I tell them, smiling. "The Secret Sisters Club."

"The Secret Sisters Club," they both say at the same time, waiting for me to continue.

"Yeah. We'll be a gossip-free club and we'll only take people who are gonna have a career when they get older and we'll all help each other." I stop, nervously looking at the two of them.

Barbara nods eagerly. "Yeah, and we should tell the other girls about it. I think lots of people would want to join."

"That sounds fun," Kendall says, her eyes bright. "We should have a fee to join, so we can have a treasury to help people out with."

"Well, you shouldn't have me take care of the money," Barbara says. "I'm no good at math."

Kendall looks at Barbara, her eyebrows raised. "Yeah math is terrible."

"What?" I ask, surprised. "Math is fun! I love it."

"Easy for you to say," Kendall says bitterly.

"Well," I say, pulling my math book out of my bag, "we can work on it, if you guys want. Let's start with factoring. I think that's the first thing on the test."

The bus rumbles to a halt, its brakes hissing. The metallic clank of the door opening pulls us all away from our work.

"Well," Kendall says finally, closing her book with a thump, "we're here."

We all pack our books away and file off the bus, climbing down the high steps and into the school yard. We walk toward the building of brown brick and Barbara grins at both of us.

"I finally feel like I get it," she tells me and smiles even wider as Kendall nods. "You should do this with us all the time."

"Only if you help me with reciting my poem," I joke.

Neither of them laugh, both looking at me curiously.

"You'll do fine," Kendall tells me and I shake my head.

"I'm not sure I'll be able to recite it in front of everyone," I tell them. "I'm worried I'll stutter and mess it all up."

Barbara stops both of us, pulling us into the bathroom. "What do you mean? Try saying it to us now," she insists.

I open my mouth to recite the poem, but my throat stops moving like someone slammed the door on my lungs. They wait quietly, while I fight with my unmoving throat.

Finally, I shake my head. "I don't think I can even do this," I say, feeling defeated.

"It's alright," Kendall says, putting her hand on my shoulder. "You help us with math and we will help you with this. We'll listen to you trying to say your poem as many times as it takes."

"Thanks," I say, "but we might just sit here until we're all old and in rocking chairs."

Chapter Three
The Meeting

Barbara, Kendall, and I huddle together at the corner of the playground, sharing the concrete bench so we don't have to sit on the damp grass. It stopped raining the day I told the girls about my club idea, which was two days ago, but it still hasn't dried up.

The playground still has a few mud puddles, but the sky is so bright and blue it almost hurts my eyes. It seems beautiful, but maybe that's just because I'm happy about our first meeting.

I open the bag of Chex mix and hold it out to my friends. "A little treat for our first meeting." They scoop up handfuls and start munching, while I open my notebook. My hands shake with excitement and my stomach has that jiggly feeling like I drank too much sweet tea.

I want to make this perfect, so I try to keep my plan in mind. "All right, the first thing we have to do is welcome new members... That's us!" The three of us wiggle excitedly, making squeaky happy sounds. I can't help grinning. "Was anyone else interested in joining our club?"

Barbara shakes her head. "I didn't find anyone, but I haven't asked everyone yet."

Kendall hops in her seat excitedly. "I did! I did! There are a bunch of people who want to join us."

"Oh." I perk up even more. I didn't expect people to join our club so soon. "Where?"

Kendall looks away, waving toward one of the girls who is leaning against the monkey bars. As she gets closer, I realize it's Haley, one of the girls on the basketball team. At least ten other girls are with her.

"Secret Sisters Club?" Haley says abruptly as she reaches us and I nod. "We want in. We all have our five dollars." She looks nervous, like I'm going to tell her no or something.

I smile at her. "We have a few rules, though." As Haley and the group of other girls turn to look at me my voice suddenly goes away and I look helplessly at Kendall.

Kendall scoops the notebook out of my hands, turning to the page with the rules. "Do you promise to be positive and drama free, have a good career when you grow up, pay your five dollar fees, and come to all the club meetings?" She says it like Haley is on the stand at a trial. I almost envy her for being able to do that so easily, but she helped me when I needed her.

I collect their fees, putting them into the envelope with "treasury" written on it to join the five dollar bills Kendall, Barbara, and I already put in there. When we finally get done swearing all of the girls into the club, I hand the envelope to Barbara for safekeeping.

The envelope is snatched from between us and I spin to see who took it. Anthony, one of the boys in our class, is standing behind me holding the envelope.

He laughs, running a few steps away. When he dangles the envelope in our faces Kendall, Barbara, and I all take off after him. The other girls all stand there staring at us like they don't know what to do.

We chase him past the monkey bars and around the swings. Finally, I run around the other side, and as he turns away from me to run the other way, he almost runs into Kendall. Barbara and Kendall grab him and I snatch the envelope from his hand.

"Nice try."

He yanks himself away from my two friends and spits on the ground. "Maybe if you hadn't ganged up on me with your Barbie and Ken-doll."

Kendall looks hurt and Barbara puts her arms around Kendall's shoulders. The boys all started calling Kendall that last year and she always gets upset about it. My chest feels hot as I watch Kendall almost cry.

"That joke is a little old. What are you, a third grader?" I shoot back, hoping he will leave her alone.

He looks surprised at my answer and his thick eyebrows come tightly together as he glares at me. "No."

"You've got no sense in your head," I tell him, turning and walking away. Barbara and Kendall fall into step beside me and I look at them. "That's why we only want girls in our club." They laugh and it makes me warm inside to see Kendall smiling again.

As we walk away, I see Curtis playing basketball with some of the other boys. He wouldn't say something that stupid, but I can't just let him into the club. It's secret sisters, after all.

"Hey," Kendall mutters, keeping her voice low so the other girls don't hear. "You didn't stutter at all when you talked to that boy and everyone was staring at you."

I shrug. "I was defending my sisters. I guess I didn't think about it."

Barbara smiles. "Maybe that's how we can help you with your problem. Let's try it again after school."

"I'll think about the poem later. Right now we have to get back to our meeting," I say, then hand the notebook to Kendall. "Here, all you have to do is follow what I've written in here. It's all set up for you."

Kendall tries to push the notebook back to me, but I shove it hard into her hands. Everyone is staring and I can feel my face getting hot. I look at her, begging her with my mind. Finally, she shakes her head in disappointment and turns to the rest of the club. "Let's recite the club pledge," she says brightly, pretending nothing happened.

She holds up the book so everyone can see the big words I have written on the page. They follow along, but I don't need to look. I know the pledge by heart.

We all recite it together. "I pledge that I will make a difference and be a better person, hold a great career and show love for all my sisters without drama or gossip, from now until forever." The pledge makes my spine tingle and I can't keep a grin off my face as the last word of the pledge rings in my ears.

Forever. This whole group will be part of that pledge for the rest of our lives and we won't ever be alone again.

"Now," Kendall continues to read from the notebook, "we have a few things we want to get done as a club. We have a club newspaper planned." She pauses as the girls jump up and down, clapping excitedly. They all look as happy as I feel. "Can I see a show of hands for people who are interested in writing for our newspaper?"

Everyone raises their hand and Kendall laughs a little. She has her hand up, too, and she looks at me and Barbara. The paper will be great with this many people writing articles.

"We will have more information on the paper during the next meeting," Kendall informs us, then turns the page. "Next, we have a club badge. We will pass it out and you should wear it to show that you are part of our club. You can put it on your back-pack if you want."

I pull the badges out of my bag and I am suddenly glad that I made way too many of the little yellow bows. They are really just ribbons I tied onto safety pins in a pretty bow shape, but they were so fun to make that I got carried away. Barbara and I pass them out and when we are done I only have seven left. Everyone pins them proudly onto their shirts as I put the bag away and fasten my own pin. We look good.

"Last order of business, we plan to have birthday parties for our club members. Every month that one of our members has a birthday, we will celebrate it sometime that month. If there is more than one birthday in the same month, we will hold one party for all of them together. We will pay for the parties with our club treasury and donations and all of the club members will be invited. Are there any birthdays this month?" Kendall's straight, shiny black hair swings as she looks back and forth at everyone.

Barbara raises her hand, her dark eyes shining. "I do."

Haley clears her throat loudly. "We can hold the parties at my house," she announces, lifting her pointed chin. "There's plenty of room there and my mom would be glad to let us come decorate."

Kendall nods and opens her mouth to say something, but Haley keeps talking.

"We don't have any officers for the club," she says, her upturned nose raised so high that we can almost see straight up her nostrils. "Are we going to do that or..."

The bell rings, its shrieking sound cutting through whatever Haley had to say. All of the girls turn toward the school again, to head inside for class.

I stand. It's easier to talk to everyone when they are turned away. "We'll have elections tomorrow, at the next meeting at recess." By the time people turn around to listen, I'm done talking. I quickly scoop up my backpack and follow everyone else through the big glass doors of the school.

The club has gone better than I thought. It's growing fast and we have so many things we will be able to do. I hug myself to hold in all my joy and keep it from exploding my chest. My big idea is the answer to all of our problems, I can feel it.

"All right," Kendall says, reading my notebook. We already added two more members and hurried through the pledge so we could get to the elections. "We will hold these elections by nomination. Anyone who wants to be president has to be nominated by one other person. You can't nominate yourself. If you get nominated to be a candidate and you don't want to be, you can decline. After we have all the candidates, we will all vote. Okay?" She looks up into the group of nodding heads. "First, we are going to hold elections for club president."

My hand shoots up first. Kendall and a few other girls have their hands up, but Kendall nods at me to go first. I call out, "I nominate Kendall for president."

Kendall shakes her head. "Thanks, but I don't want to be president. I nominate Destiny for club president. It was your idea and you're the one who writes out the meetings."

I can feel my face getting hot and I shrug weakly. I'll never be able to hold a meeting on my own, but I guess it makes sense. I will be sure to nominate Kendall for vice president.

Most of the other girls have put their hands down. I wonder if they were going to nominate me too. From the way they all smile at me, I think they were.

"Come on!" someone whispers sharply beside me and I look over to see Haley smiling innocently beside Trinity.

Trinity raises her hand in the air. "I nominate Haley for club president!"

Haley looks surprised and thanks Trinity, pretending everyone around her didn't just hear her whisper. Kendall looks doubtful, but I shake my head at her. I thought at least one person

would ask someone to nominate them. I didn't expect it to be Haley, but I guess I should have. Haley always wants to be at the front of the line or head of the class.

"Any other nominations?"

"Nope!" Haley calls, two spots of red on her toffee-colored cheeks.

No one else answers, so Kendall nods. "Okay, everyone gets one vote. You have to vote for one of these two, you can't just decide not to vote. Raise your hand now if you vote for Haley."

A bunch of hands go up and I can't tell if it's more than half. Kendall's face is blank as she counts all of the votes and writes them down in my notebook.

"Okay, hands down." Everyone's hands lower obediently. "Raise your hand now if you vote for Destiny."

Hands go up again and this time I raise mine. I don't mind Haley, but I really want this club to go well and she doesn't always do things the way I'd like. Kendall and Barbara have raised their hands, too, and I smile at them. Kendall doesn't look at me, but Barbara reaches with her other hand to squeeze my shoulder.

Kendall finally lifts her head from her notebook. "By five votes, the new president of the Secret Sisters Club is..."

We all wait, holding our breath as she pauses dramatically.

"Destiny!"

There is a big cheer and everyone claps, even the people who voted for Haley. I can't keep my grin from spreading across my face and I hold my cheeks in my hands happily. Then I raise my hand. "I'll try again," I say. "Kendall for vice president."

"Hold your horses, I didn't get there yet." Kendall says, but her eyes are all shiny. She seems happy about this one. "Any other nominations?"

I turn to see Haley nudge Trinity, but Trinity shakes her head. No one else raises their hand, even though Kendall waits for even longer than she did for the president nominations.

"All right, I guess I'm vice president." Kendall has a smile as big as mine.

Haley sniffs angrily and a few people turn to look at her. She tosses her curly dark hair, her hands on her hips. "Shouldn't more people be involved in this club? I mean, I brought a lot of people to the club. I should be part of it somehow."

Kendall looks at me, then down at the notebook. "We have some more elections coming up," she tells Haley. "Maybe you should try for one of those?"

Haley only sniffs again in response, so Kendall starts taking nominations for secretary. When Barbara wins the spot, Haley seems almost ready to burst. I slide up next to Kendall, pull a pen out of my backpack and write in a quick note in the notebook that says "public relations."

Kendall perks up immediately. "Public relations officer, anyone nominate someone for that?"

Trinity nominates Haley again, and since she is the only one chosen, she gets the position automatically. She seems to calm down because of that and we all let out a breath we hadn't realized we were holding.

Next is treasurer. Haley nominates Trinity and Barbara nominates Carlise because she has a cash box at home she can use for the club. Haley looks like she is going to burn holes in Barbara with her eyes and Trinity looks like she will cry.

I had never thought people would get so upset about not being club officers. Kendall looks super nervous and I know I have to do something. If I don't, there will be a fight over who is treasurer and my whole club could go up in flames.

I step up next to Kendall and take a deep breath. I look at Barbara. She's been helping me try to recite my poem and I've found out that when I look at just one person I stutter a lot less. She stares back at me, her big brown eyes wide.

"We should have two treasurers," I say loudly, looking only at Barbara. "It's a lot of money and we don't want someone accusing the treasurer of stealing. So, two."

I don't know how I managed to get through the whole thing without stuttering, but I did it. As I back up, amazed with myself, everyone becomes silent.

Finally, Kendall shrugs. "Let's vote on it. Everyone who wants to have two treasurers?" She raises her hand.

The whole group of us, even the two treasurers, reaches their hands high. Haley seems much happier and even smiles a little as she looks around.

"Looks like we don't have to count," I say without thinking and the laugh that goes through the group makes me smile too.

Part II:
Secret Sisters Club

Chapter Four
The Party

The doorbell rings inside the big brick house in front of me and I wait. I brought Barbara's gift in a pretty gift bag for our first club birthday party. I kind of wish it was a bigger bag, so I could hide behind it. I'm not sure why I'm so nervous. I just keep getting this feeling that someone is going to jump out and tell me it's too good to be true and then the club will be over.

To keep my mind off it, I look at the house. It's not as big as it looked when I first walked up, but it's bigger than mine. The windows all have shutters over them, but there are pretty window boxes with poinsettias in them for Christmas. The door opens and I try not to jump. Haley's mother waves me in with a big smile on her face. She's wearing a dress with even more poinsettias on it.

"It's so wonderful you girls are doing this!" she tells me as I step into the house. The living room has a lot of pictures and even more poinsettias. I try to remember what Momma always says when we go to a party.

"Thank you for having us, Mrs..." What is Haley's last name again? For a second I panic and I can feel the stutter forming in the back of my throat.

"Davis," she finishes for me, then pushes me gently toward the back of the house. "I'm Mrs. Davis and Haley and Curtis are in the kitchen."

I stop dead in my tracks, butterflies coming to life in my stomach at the sound of Curtis' name. "C-Curtis?"

Mrs. Davis doesn't seem to notice my stutter and she nods. "He's such a good boy. He and Haley are friends. He offered to help with your little party."

We get to the kitchen, where Haley and Curtis are sitting on the counter next to each other. Curtis jumps down and gives me a gleaming white smile with his perfect teeth, but Haley looks like she'd rather I wasn't there.

Before we can say anything, the doorbell rings again and Mrs. Davis hurries away to get it. A few seconds later Trinity, Carlise, and Kendall come into the kitchen.

"Hey guys!" Kendall calls cheerfully as she pulls some balloons out of one of Trinity's grocery bags. "I met them at the door. They got a lot of decorations and cupcakes."

"Good," I say, glad for Kendall's interruption. "Let's get started."

Pop! Pop! Pop!

Three balloons explode as Kendall runs through them. The others balloons scatter like scared puppies. "I love balloon bowling!" she laughs and everyone else laughs, too.

I want to laugh with them, but we have been working on this a while and Kendall's new balloon bowling game is popping as many balloons as we blow up. The cupcakes are still in their cardboard box and the decorations are still in Trinity's grocery bag. I take a deep breath.

"Okay, guys, that's fun, but we have to get this stuff done," I say, staring at the fridge and imagining that I'm alone. When I finally look at Kendall, her golden cheeks are a little red from embarrassment, but she nods.

"Just tell us what to do, Destiny," she says and everyone turns to look at me.

I can feel my face getting hot. Kendall knows I don't want to give orders. She's probably upset that I fussed at her. I try to smile at her, but she just waits. Finally, I take another breath. "Kendall, start hanging balloons. Trinity and Carlise, you keep blowing up balloons for her."

I turn to Haley, who has her hands on her hips. Something about the way she raises her eyebrows at me makes me mad, so I give her an order too. "Haley, go hang the happy birthday sign."

Everyone, but Curtis, starts working. He is looking at me with a smile in his hazel eyes. "Anything for me to do?" he asks, but before I can get nervous again Haley steps between him and me.

"You can help me hang the sign," she says in her most demanding voice. I hope I didn't sound like that.

I nod. "He's the only one tall enough anyway!" I joke, then hurry away to get the cupcakes arranged.

We all stand back, enjoying the view of our work. Yellow balloons for our club colors and purple ones for Barbara's favorite color are tied up all over the living room and the kitchen. The cupcakes and Barbara's present sit next to each other on the kitchen table, which is covered with a pretty yellow tablecloth. The whole house looks like a giant party room and Kendall sighs happily.

"We did it," she says, just as the doorbell rings.

I nod, hoping Barbara will like her present.

More people flood into the house, all of the club members and a few girls I don't know. I turn to Kendall. "Just in time!" I laugh. "But who are the other people?"

She shrugs. "A few other girls who want to join our Secret Sisters Club."

"More?" I can't believe our club is growing so fast.

"Yeah. Trinity put the word out about the club party, so maybe a few more people can join today."

I spot a familiar face in the group. Her dark, curly hair is pulled back into a headband and her big brown eyes shift around as she laughs at something the girl next to her said. "That's Tracey," I say, pointing. "She gossips a lot. We don't want a gossip in our club."

Kendall frowns. "Are you sure she gossips? Maybe we should let everyone vote on who should be in the club."

"Maybe," I say, not sure. I don't want to risk having the club turn into a popularity contest. If our club members only vote for their favorite people, that would be bad.

Finally, I see Barbara, dressed all in purple with her little yellow ribbon pinned to her shirt. Kendall sees her, too, and starts jumping up and down and waving.

"Wow," she says as she gets closer to us. "I thought it would just be a small party!"

I can't contain my excitement. "Attention!" I shout and the room gets quiet. They all turn to look at me and my throat closes up again. I look to Kendall for help, but she just looks confused.

To my relief, Barbara steps forward. "Thanks! I really love this party!"

I nudge Kendall. "Happy birthday?" I mutter and she nods in understanding.

We all sing happy birthday to Barbara, and as soon as the song ends, I put her gift in her hands. We all watch quietly as Barbara pulls out first a notebook and then a pretty pen, both of them purple and yellow.

"Wow. This is so great everyone!" Barbara exclaims, her eyes shining.

"Now you won't have to take notes on something boring!" I tell her, wiggling in excitement.

"All right!" Kendall chirps. "Time for cupcakes."

"The new softball coach is so funny!" Tracey giggles, leaning against Curtis. She, Kendall, Trinity, and I are all on the softball team and we are sitting down together to talk while everyone else plays pin the tail on the donkey.

I had come over to make sure that Tracey didn't gossip, but she seems more interested in Curtis than telling tales. I try to be relieved instead of jealous.

As we laugh at Trinity's imitation of the new softball coach when she signals us to steal a base, Barbara comes up behind me.

"Hey guys, what y'all talking about?" she asks, bouncing up and down.

I shake my head. "You wouldn't get it," I tell her. "Softball team only."

Barbara looks hurt. "Well, Curtis isn't on the softball team and he gets it," she points out. "Maybe you could try?"

Trinity crosses her arms. "Why are you being so nosy? This is an A-B conversation. You should C your way out of it!"

Everyone laughs nervously, not sure what to do. Barbara's lower lip shakes and I reach for her arm, but she pulls away. She walks away and sits on a stool near the front door.

"Is she crying?" Kendall asks, peering at her.

"I'm not sure," I say, feeling guilty. I look at Trinity. "Why did you say that?" I ask, but she shrugs and won't look at me.

"It's okay," Kendall tells me, turning away. "She'll get over it."

"It doesn't matter if she will," I say, standing up and clenching my fists. Then I point at Barbara. "Club meeting, over there."

We walk over to Barbara and she smiles in a weird way at me. "Hey Destiny," she says, her voice shaking.

"We're sorry, Barbara," I say and she waves her hand.

"I'm fine. You worry too much!" she laughs, but I don't believe her.

"We're just going to talk for a while," I tell her.

She tries to wave me away again, but we all stay. I make sure that she stays talking until, finally, she is smiling.

✧ ✧ ✧

Someone taps me on the shoulder and I turn. One of the girls who joined the club a few days ago smiles at me, the small gap in her two front teeth showing.

"Hey Julianna," I say, smiling at her. "What's up?"

"We were thinking," she says, then pauses and shrugs, looking down. "I mean, some new people..." She stops, then scratches the back of her neck like she's nervous.

I look at Barbara and smile. "I think we should have a meeting to vote. Let everyone have a say in who should be in the club."

Barbara smiles back at me. "That sounds good."

Trinity hops up from her spot next to Barbara. "I have the cash box. We can get started now."

When I nod, they all hurry off to tell everyone else. I wait for everyone to settle down for the meeting, watching my friends. Maybe it's best that we all have a say in how the club runs, so no one feels left out like Barbara did. We're all secret sisters together, and as long as we have each other, I'm sure everything else will turn out fine.

Chapter Five
Big News

✧ ✧ ✧

"All right," I say, scooping up my backpack and backing toward the door of Mrs. Sparks' classroom. I had met her early before school to get an interview about the upcoming school play.

"Don't forget to mention that we're still looking for someone to play the part of Jack," she tells me for the seventh time, smiling at me behind those big glasses of hers. Her long skirt swishes as she turns away to erase the writing that is still on the chalkboard from the day before.

"Yes, ma'am, I'll be sure to mention that." I push open the door and step into the long, gray hallway. It is still early; the halls are almost deserted. Almost.

Tracey sees me and starts walking toward me, but I hurry into the library. She was so upset when we voted to keep her out of the club. We told her that if she stops gossiping, she might still be able to join and that we would vote on it at the next meeting. Every day since then she has found me and talked to me forever about how hard she is trying to stop gossiping and has asked me to hold a meeting to vote her into the club. I like Tracey, but I have work to do.

I hurry to one of the study desks in the corner, behind one of the big shelves. Tracey usually doesn't follow me into the library because she's not allowed to talk in here. I pull out my newspaper writing checklist and look at it. I'm so excited about this newspaper I could jump up and down.

I've already written two articles for the newspaper and this interview for the school play will be my third. Now, I just need to type them. I assigned everyone in the club articles to write and they are all due today. I can't wait to read them.

I slam my locker closed and sigh unhappily. It's after lunch, already, and people have been avoiding me all day. I wonder if this is how Tracey feels.

Only Barbara gave me her article about head colds. Everyone else either says they forgot about their articles or hurries away when I come up to talk to them about it. Even Kendall has been avoiding me, but she's by her locker now. She can't get away. I walk up to her, putting on my biggest smile and pretending not to notice that she is staring into her locker to avoid looking at me.

"Hey, Kendall. Have you finished that article about the new books in the library?" I wait patiently for an answer.

She shakes her razor-straight black hair away from her face and squints, making her narrow eyes seem even smaller. "Article?" she asks, like she has no idea what I'm talking about.

"Yeah, remember we were each writing a newspaper article? That's due today."

"Oh right, that." Kendall clears her throat. "Well, I've just had a lot of homework and softball practice..." She pauses and finally looks at me. "I just forgot. I can get it done later, okay?"

I cross my arms. "No one but Barbara has given me anything and I did three articles already. How come nobody else can get theirs done?"

Kendall throws her hands in the air. "It's just a stupid paper, what do you care?"

I clench my fists at my sides and have to try hard to keep from shouting at her. "I care because I want a club paper, not some boring little newsletter no one wants to read. If I have to, I'll write the whole thing myself."

Before Kendall can answer, I spin on my heel and stalk away. She'll wish she put her article in my paper because everyone will read it and love it. I don't need anyone to help me with it. I'll do it myself.

"Destiny!" Mrs. Elena snaps and I jump. She is standing at the front of the class with her hands on her hips and everyone is looking straight at me. "I've been trying to get your attention for the last two minutes." Her face is crinkled with anger. "It's the last class of the day and you have ten minutes left. What are you doing that's so important you can't pay attention for ten more minutes?"

My face gets hot and I wish I could shrink down so small no one could see me. I had been working on newspaper articles during all of the classes that day. No one else noticed, but I got so involved that I never noticed she was talking to me. "Uh...," I say and after a few seconds Mrs. Elena sighs and takes my notebook from me.

"See me after class," she says, handing me some loose-leaf paper to take notes on. "Haley, come forward to recite your poem."

As Haley swishes past me to the front of the class, I sink down in my chair and hope she doesn't give me a detention.

"This is a poem about my puppy and my favorite flower, sunflowers!" she says all sicky-sweet and I try not to groan. Maybe I could go do my detention now.

As soon as Haley finishes her poem, the bell rings and everyone jumps up to leave. A few students go to Mrs. Elena's desk to ask her a question and I wait glumly in my seat.

"Hey, so what were you working on? It looked really important."

I look up to see Julianna standing next to my desk, her books in her arms. She is one of our club members and my nervousness about the talk with Mrs. Elena turns into anger. If she and the other club members had done what I told them to, I wouldn't be in trouble now.

"Newspaper stuff," I tell her, crossing my arms. "No one's turned in their articles, so I have to do all of them. Have you done your article?" I've forgotten what I gave her to write. Something about makeup, I think.

Julianna looks at the floor, ashamed. I can't help feeling a little better. At least someone feels bad about it. "I haven't done it yet," she admits. "Which article were you working on?"

The other students have left and Mrs. Elena is walking toward us, but Julianna doesn't seem to notice. "It's about the new books in the library," I tell her quickly, hoping she will go away so Mrs. Elena won't start the embarrassing conversation in front of her.

"Oh," Julianna says brightly. "I wish I was doing that one. I'd be a lot more interested in something like that."

"Something like what?" Mrs. Elena asks, settling into a desk.

We tell her all about the newspaper and she listens quietly. Finally, she folds her hands in front of her and asks, "Why are you writing all of the articles?"

"I shouldn't be," I tell her bitterly. "It's just, no one else will do the articles I told them to do."

Julianna clears her throat. "Maybe if we could choose them," she says, then shrugs and looks away.

"If you want to write the rest of the library article, you can," I tell her. I had just started on it anyway.

Julianna nods happily. "Hey, why don't you let other people choose their articles too? I'm a lot more excited about this one."

"I never thought about it, I guess."

Mrs. Elena looks at me with a weird look on her face. "Is that why you weren't paying attention in class?"

My face burns even more and I get a tight feeling in the back of my throat, like when I'm about to stutter. I don't want to say anything in case I stutter, so I just nod.

Mrs. Elena gets my notebook and brings it to me. "Take this and let everyone pick their own topic. And stop doing other work in my class, even if it is writing."

✦ ✦ ✦

Later, while I'm teaching Kendall and Barbara fraction multiplication in Barbara's kitchen, I look up from our books. "Hey, what do you two think about each person choosing which article they want to write, instead of one being assigned?"

Barbara shrugs. "I already handed mine in, but I wouldn't mind writing another about something interesting. That first article was boring."

"Yours was boring?" Kendall exclaims, propping her elbows on the table. "Mine was about new books in the library." She drops her head on the table and starts snoring loudly.

I laugh along with Barbara, but I'm a little surprised. I had no idea it would be such a big deal. "Well, I think we should call a meeting and get those articles re-assigned. What do you guys think?"

Kendall's head pops up. "Good idea. And while we're paused on our math lesson, it's time for you to recite your poem to us again. Remember, relax your throat as much as you can and try to look at our noses if you have trouble with looking us in the eye."

Barbara puts her pencil down, too, and I groan. "But we haven't gotten through even five example problems."

"That's okay," Barbara says. "We'll do ten before your next poetry reading. How's that?"

I sigh and concentrate on my breathing, while I recite the poetry for them.

Chapter Six

Tracey

I can't stop looking at the club newspaper, even though I should pay attention to the club meeting. We finished the paper less than a day after I allowed everyone to choose their own topics. I still can't believe it worked so well. I had stayed up all night to finish it, but it was the prettiest newspaper I had ever seen.

"...next order of business is new members," I hearKendall saying, her voice high and clear as she stands with her fingertips resting on the table in front of us. She has been leading our meetings in the library every weekend, in the little meeting room in the back. I've been working on my poem with Barbara and Kendall every day and I'm almost ready to recite it, but I still think Kendall should run the club meetings. She says I can do it by myself, but I'm not sure. I write the whole order of the meeting out for her so she doesn't have to think of things to say, but the thought of standing in front of the rows of girls in front of me and talking makes my throat freeze up again.

Kendall glances at me as Tracey stands up to ask for membership. I smile at Tracey, then flip to the notebook page about what Kendall should say when there are new members who want to join. There have been a lot, although we don't have new members every meeting anymore. We have seventy-two members, nearly all of the girls in our school. Tracey is the only one left who has been trying to join.

"Rule 1, every member of the Secret Sisters Club has to be a girl," Kendall reads and I watch Tracey. Her almond skin is a little bit lighter than mine and her wild curly hair makes a pretty pouf around her head. Her big brown eyes are sad, like she doesn't expect to be let in the club this time either. Why does she even try anymore? "Rule 2, every member of the Secret Sisters Club must be positive and drama-free."

Tracey flinches at that and I feel sorry for her. Kendall's hands tighten around the notebook. She must have seen it too.

"Rule 3, every member of the Secret Sisters Club must have a future career," she continues. "Rule 4, everyone must pay five dollars to join the Secret Sisters Club, and Rule 5, every member must attend Secret Sisters Club meetings."

The quiet after Kendall finishes reading the rules sounds loud. All seventy-two of the Secret Sisters Club members are watching Tracey, but she is staring at the floor.

"I do gossip," Tracey admits finally, her eyes full of tears. "But I've been trying to stop. I haven't done it all week. I promise if you let me in the club I'll never do it again."

Kendall crosses her arms over her chest and opens her mouth, but I can't stand it any longer. Tracey looks so miserable and alone up there. I clear my throat quickly and stand up, before I get too scared and reconsider. Kendall's eyes get wide and she sits down to let me talk.

"If you work half as hard at being a good club member as you do at spreading gossip, you'll be the best we've ever had," I joke.

I feel a little bad because it sounds kinda mean, but Tracey laughs louder than anyone, so I guess it's okay.

Before I have a chance to say anything else, Haley stands up and glares at Tracey. Tracey's smile disappears and she looks more sad and scared than ever. "It's in our rules, you can't gossip and be part of our club," she says, her voice almost a growl. "We can't change that just because we want to let you in."

I sit down, surprised by Haley's outburst, and Barbara leans toward me from the other side of Kendall. All the girls who were quiet before start muttering to one another, just as confused as I am.

"Tracey was flirting with Curtis," Barbara tells Kendall and me and my stomach does a little flop at the sound of his name. I had been so worried about the newspaper that I forgot about him, but hearing his name makes the butterflies come back.

"Curtis?" I whisper back, pretending not to know who she's talking about.

Kendall rolls her eyes as the muttering gets louder around us. "You know, that guy you get all googly-eyed about."

My face gets hot when Barbara smiles and nods. "Yeah, that guy. He and Haley are dating."

I nod. Haley must be so upset because she's worried Tracey will steal her man. I don't like the idea of Tracey flirting with Curtis either, but that's not a good reason to keep her out of the Secret Sisters Club. I stand up again.

The other girls have gotten so loud that I have to smack the notebook against the table to get everyone to quiet down. Finally, they calm down enough that I can talk. I smile at Tracey, who seems like she's holding her breath. That freezing feeling starts up in my throat, but I force it to smooth out just like I've been doing for poetry practice.

"We can't let you into the club, just yet," I tell her, but I hold up a finger as her lips begin to tremble. "But! I think we should make you a probationary member. You can join today and we'll all agree to talk about this again at the next meeting. If you haven't gossiped or caused drama, then you can join for real." I thump back into my seat with my face burning. I didn't stutter, but all those people looking at me was so weird. I can't tell if I liked it or not.

Tracey is grinning at me and nodding so hard I'm worried her head will fly off. "I won't, I promise. You'll see. This will be great!"

"Shouldn't we vote on this?" Haley sniffed loudly, her hands on her hips.

"Of course," Kendall says in her best sweet as sugar voice and we all vote. All the girls now have to close their eyes while they vote, so Barbara and I are the only ones left to take count. We both look at each other, worried. The vote is split almost in half.

I count the list of "yea" and "nay" votes two more times, just to be sure. Tracey is only in the club by three votes, but she's in. I am glad that we made her close her eyes for the voting, because she would have been upset by how many people didn't want her to join. Most of those people are Haley's group, which makes me a little nervous. What if they decide to take over one day?

They didn't today, though. I hand the vote count to Kendall, who smiles. "Congratulations, Tracey. You are a probationary member of the Secret Sisters Club."

"Mrs. Sparks?" the principal, Mr. Gabriel says, peeking in through a crack in the classroom door. He waves her out into the hallway.

"Read the next scene of Romeo and Juliet," she says as she hurries out the door and everyone except Barbara and me groans.

I find it hard to pay attention to the reading. Mr. Gabriel never comes into our classroom, unless something is very wrong. Is someone in trouble?

The other kids seem to be thinking the same thing, because a few of them get up and put their ears to the door. Before they have a chance to listen, Mrs. Sparks comes back in. Instead of fussing at the students for being out of their desks, she seems pale and upset.

"Close your books and line up," she says, "We're heading to the gymnasium. Mr. Gabriel has an announcement." We line up like we're going to a pep rally.

We file slowly through the hall alongside other students and all the teachers have the same look. Mrs. Elena has streaks of mascara running down her face. A knot starts to grow in my stomach when I see that.

We all find our seats on the bleachers and there is an odd quiet as everyone looks around, not sure what to do. All of the Secret Sisters Club is in a group, clustered around Kendall, Barbara, and me. Barbara grabs my hand. We hold tight, waiting as Mr. Gabriel looks around and rubs his bald head.

"All right, everyone here? Good." Mr. Gabriel takes a deep breath, holding a large stack of papers in his dark hands. He lifts them in front of him like a shield as he reads them. "It is with great sorrow that I tell you all of the death of one of your schoolmates." We all look around and a low mutter comes from hundreds of mouths as he continues. "Miss Tracey Jonest, in your eighth grade class, died in a four-wheeler accident this past weekend." I put my hand to my mouth and the knot in my stomach seems to drop into my knees. "There will be a wake for her this Saturday and all of her class mates and friends are invited to attend."

Mr. Gabriel allows us to stay in the gym while we talk about Tracey and the Secret Sisters Club all cries together. Haley looks like she is going to pass out. I can't help thinking that in only a few more days Tracey would have been a member of the club. It seems like a few other people are thinking the same thing.

"I wish we had just taken her stupid five dollars and let her in the club," Kendall says and everyone, including Haley, nods sadly.

Something about their faces gives me an idea. "Hey," I say. "We can't change it, but what about if we took donations for her family?"

Barbara raises her eyebrows. "That might be nice. It was really expensive for my family when we had to bury my G-maw. We could go around and ask people if they would donate, too."

"Let's go check with Mrs. Sparks," Kendall says and the whole Secret Sisters Club goes to ask her.

Two days later, Barbara, Kendall, and I stand outside the door of Tracey's house. We all have black clothing on for the wake and the big envelope in my hand holds more than 170 dollars. It's so big that it bulges, but it doesn't feel like nearly enough to make up for Tracey. Kendall and Barbara and I are skipping our math and poetry reciting work for this, but it's worth it. None of us can concentrate on our lessons anyway; we keep thinking of Tracey.

Tracey's momma opens the door and my throat closes up again, but Kendall is ready. "Mrs. Jonest," she says, stepping in front of me. "We're friends of Tracey's and we wanted to tell you how sorry we are to hear about what happened." She takes a deep breath, then turns to me.

"We went around," I tell her, lifting the envelope for Mrs. Jonest to take, "and collected for her funeral, to help with the costs. We want you to have this."

Mrs. Jonest looks like a taller version of Tracey, even with the pouf of hair around her head. She takes the envelope and doesn't even look inside, but steps forward to give us all a big hug. When she pulls away, there are tears sparkling in her eyes.

"I'm glad to hear she has such good friends," she says, then pulls the door wider. "Please come on in."

Part III:
A New Idea

Chapter Seven
Changes

I slouch in the bus seat, putting my feet up on the back of the chair in front of me. It's the last week of school, and even though the sun is just rising, I feel like I'm melting in the heat. I can't wait for summer. I close my eyes, dreaming of pool parties.

After a while, someone thumps down into the seat next to me. I open my eyes to see Curtis looking at me. I never noticed before how long and curly his eyelashes are. I can't catch my breath for a few seconds, but I jump and pretend like he scared me.

"Sorry about that," he says, but he's grinning. "I thought maybe I could hang out with you for a while."

The swirly, butterfly feeling in my stomach turns into a rushing waterfall and I can't help smiling. Curtis wants to hang out with me! "I don't mind," I say, trying to be cool. "Haley might, though."

"Haley and I broke up." He pauses, looking around, even though we were the only ones on the bus. "Can you keep a secret?"

I nod eagerly, feeling a little hot in my cheeks because of how close we are sitting. His leg is almost touching mine.

"She always tried to keep me from talking to people. I hated not being able to hang out with my friends or talk to her friends. So, I told her we couldn't be together."

"Well, you can talk to my friends," I say, and to my surprise, I giggle at him. "But you have to sit on the side near the window, so I can talk to them easier."

When Barbara gets on the bus, she sees Curtis holding my hand and her eyebrows shoot up so high I'm afraid they will fly off. "Hey Destiny," she says and stops by my seat. She seems to think about taking a seat farther back and I panic. I like Curtis and his hand feels good in mine, but I don't want to lose my friends.

"Hey Barbara!" I say, trying to think of something to make her stay. "We have so much to talk about!"

Barbara sits in the seat across from us and I stop myself right before letting out a sigh of relief. "I wanted to tell you, I am going to my grandma's house all summer. I won't be around to go to meetings."

"Oh," I say. Barbara loves her grandma's house, but the summer is always less fun without her. I'll still have Kendall, but it's never the same. I don't want to make her feel bad, so I smile and shrug. "That's alright. I'm sure I can prep for the meetings. I'll miss you, though."

Curtis' hand tightens on mine as he leans toward Barbara. He smells like freshly cut grass and I can feel my face getting hot again. "I would help with the meeting prep, but I have a basket-ball camp to go to this summer. I'll be gone a lot, too."

Barbara giggles. "The club is just for girls anyway, silly."

"Oh," he says, but he grins like he already knew that. "Bummer."

Kendall startles us all by falling into her seat next to Barbara with a flump, her arms crossed over her chest. "Hey guys," she says in the dullest voice ever.

Barbara and I look at each other and shrug, but it's Curtis who asks, "What's wrong, Kendall?"

She glares at him like she's not going to answer, but after a few seconds she shrugs. "We're losing the house we rented. The guy who rented it to us is finally selling it." Her eyes fill with tears and her lower lip begins to shake. Her landlord had been trying to sell the house they were renting since before the Christmas holidays. "We have a new place to live," her voice starts to go higher, like she's going to cry, "but it's in another state and my mom has a job there and..."

Her voice turns into a squeaking wail. She drops her head into her hands, crying as her sleek black hair falls forward around her face. I let go of Curtis' hand to hug Kendall and Barbara pats her awkwardly on the shoulder.

"I'll have... have to go...," she cries in a strangled voice, then sniffs, "to a new... school." She lifts her head so we can see her deep brown eyes all puffy and lined with red. "I w-won't see you..."

I shake my head. "You'll still see us," I tell her, not sure how I will make it work. "We can talk on the phone and I'll walk to your house to visit if I have to."

Kendall smiles. "You always know how to make me feel better," she says, even though she is still sniffing. "I don't know what I will do without you guys."

"I dunno what I'm gonna do without you, either," I tell her seriously. "Who will run the meetings when you leave?"

"Why don't you?" Curtis asks and I shrug, embarrassed.

"She's worried she'll stutter," Kendall tells him and I'm not sure if I'm grateful she explained for me or upset she told him. "She doesn't do it anymore, though."

I shake my head. "Just because I recited my poem alright doesn't mean that I can lead meetings." I can't help the warm feeling that rises inside when I think of reciting my poem, though. Even though it was months ago, I still haven't gotten over it.

The room had been so quiet after I finished, a flawless performance without even one stutter. All the other students were looking at me with wide eyes full of admiration. Mrs. Elena, raising her eyebrows and saying softly, "Very, very good. I'd definitely like to publish your poem on the website…"

"…what do you think of that, Destiny?" Kendall was saying and I shook myself.

"What?"

"I was saying, you should make someone else vice president if you really don't want to run meetings. Haley might want to do it. She's been asking if she can run a meeting for a while."

I frown. Haley hadn't said anything to me and I'm the president. "I don't know if I trust Haley."

"All right, what about Barbara? I know she's secretary, but she's good at talking."

Curtis laughs. "Sounds like you're getting a promotion, Barbara."

I tilt my head, considering. "That's not a bad idea, but we'd need someone for the summer while she's gone at her grandma's house. Whatcha think, Barbara?"

Barbara is already shaking her head when I turn to look at her. "Nuh-uh, not me," she insists. "I like being secretary. I don't want to be vice president or president or treasurer or anything else. I'm fine with the way I am right now."

"All right, all right," I say with a laugh, holding my hands up in surrender.

Kendall looks at Barbara like she's grown an extra head. "What do you mean you don't want anything else? You actually like being secretary?"

"Of course I do," Barbara answers, crossing her arms over her chest. "You like being vice president, don't you?"

"Yeah."

"Then what's different about it?"

I laugh. "You guys look so funny when you argue about stuff like that. Everyone has their own things they like and dislike, nothing wrong with that."

"I guess so," Kendall admits. "I still think Barbara should do it."

"Well, that isn't an option," Barbara snaps. The rest of us jump. She doesn't get mad a lot, but when she does she's always really snippy. "Even if I wanted to, it wouldn't work for this summer, so maybe we should focus on fixing the problem."

There is a long, long pause while I listen to the sounds of the bus bumping over the street. Finally Barbara mutters, "Sorry."

"It's okay." Kendall shrugs, then turns to me. "Don't worry, Destiny, you'll think of something. You always do."

I lean back in my seat and Curtis smiles at me encouragingly as his hand tightens around mine. So many things are changing, I'm not sure I can keep up.

Chapter Eight
Dollar Thief

I can't believe the year has gone by so fast. It's already the end of the year awards ceremony, and as I step out of the car and walk with Momma, my hands shake. I'm not sure why. Maybe it's because I'll be officially a ninth grader soon and that scares me a little. My grandma, Lucy-Belle, always used to say that growing up happened too fast, but I never knew what she meant until now.

We slowly file into the gymnasium for the event. Even though it's been decorated with nice tables and a podium it somehow reminds me of the day we found out about Tracey. My stomach flips and I clench my fists at my side.

We walk past rows of tables. Ahead of us, too far away to call over the buzz of people chattering, Julianna waves at me. I wave back, wondering if I can trust her to be vice president of the club next year. She did help a lot with the newspaper, but she and I haven't talked much other than that.

When she turns to follow her parents to their seating, a little green bill falls on the floor. It's five dollars. I hurry toward it, but just as I get close enough to call for Julianna, a man with a goatee scoops it up and stuffs it in his pocket. The inside of my chest gets hot and I put my hands on my hips. That money was Julianna's and he just stole it!

He tries to keep walking, but I catch him by the arm. I'm so angry I can't think of what to say, so I just blurt out the first thing that comes to my mind. "That's hers," I tell him, pointing at the table where Julianna is sitting.

The man with the goatee looks down at me, a vague smile on his face. His eyebrows scrunch up like he's confused, but I know better because his eyes are glancing around at everyone to see if they are listening. "Hello, sweetheart," he says in an oozy voice that makes me a little sick. "What's hers?"

"That money you stole. She dropped it on the ground, and I was going to give it back, but you picked it up before I could."

Goatee man's eyes widen a little and he pulls his arm out of my grip before scrunching his eyebrows up again. He puts one hand on my shoulder, too heavy for me to shrug off. "I think we just have a misunderstanding. I didn't steal any money. Go and run along now." He lifts his hand and gives me a small push back in the direction I came from.

Now I'm really mad and my face is hot as I hurry toward Mrs. Elena. Kendall and Barbara meet me along the way, but I just nod at them. I don't want them to think I'm mad at them, but I'm so upset I can't really talk.

Mrs. Elena looks up as I approach. She smiles. "Well, aren't you girls on a mission. What do you need?"

I look back to see that both Kendall and Barbara have followed me, even though I didn't talk to them. It makes me smile and the way they smile back at me calms me down a little. Then I turn to Mrs. Elena. "There's a man who stole five dollars that Julianna dropped on the floor. I tried to make him give it back, but he won't."

Mrs. Elena makes me repeat exactly what I said to him and exactly what he said back. Then she goes and has a quiet talk with Julianna before coming back to me. "Lead the way. I'll do the talking," she says and I hurry back to the man in the goatee.

He is leaning back in his chair at an empty table and he smiles as we come up to him. "Hello again," he tells me, like we had a nice talk before and nothing is wrong.

Thankfully, Mrs. Elena steps in with a smile of her own, the kind she uses when someone doesn't have their homework and pretends it's because they left it at home. "This young lady tells me that you found some money on the floor. I think I know who it belongs to. Thank you for finding it."

The man frowns, standing up and crossing his arms. "Look lady, I'll tell you the same thing I told her. I didn't take anything. That five dollars is mine."

"All right, then tell me one thing about that five dollar bill that makes you sure it's yours," Mrs. Elena challenges, leaning toward the man.

He crosses his arms tighter and shrugs. "It's kind of rumpled I guess. What's the big deal? It's five dollars."

"Really? Because the girl who dropped it says it was given to her as a reward for getting good grades and it's got a big blue splotch on it."

The man's scrunchy face turns angry and he pulls the five dollars out of his pocket, throwing it at Mrs. Elena. "Fine!" he snaps, then turns and walks out, yelling, "I didn't want to be here anyway."

Mrs. Elena unfolds the five dollar bill and there is the blue splotch, covering part of a word on the bill. "Well, let me bring this back to Julianna. Thank you, ladies. I hate to see something like that happen here."

As Mrs. Elena walks away, I look at Barbara and Kendall with a smile. They stood by me, even when they weren't sure what was going on. I'm so glad for these good friends I could burst. "He would have gotten away with it, too," I joke in my best evil-villain voice, "if it hadn't been for those pesky kids!"

As we all laugh, Curtis walks up beside me. "Hey, I saw what you did, but I couldn't get away from my folks just then. If I ever drop any money, I know who to call."

I can feel my face getting hot and shrug to hide my grin of happy pride. "If you let people get away with something small, they'll keep trying to get away with bigger and bigger things."

Curtis nods thoughtfully. "You're right." He pauses, then looks down at his feet. "Hey, so do you want to come sit with me for the awards ceremony?"

I want to, but I can't help but look at Kendall and Barbara, who seem sad that he asked. I take his arm. "Why don't you come sit with us instead?"

The four of us sit down on the bleachers with our yearbooks, all the parents sitting at the big tables. The other kids around us are loud until Mrs. Sparks takes the stand. Everybody likes Mrs. Sparks, so when she clears her throat the whole room gets quiet.

"Before we begin," she says seriously, "We lost a very special student this year..."

All of our eyes fill with tears while she talks about Tracey. Barbara and Kendall both sniffle next to me and Curtis takes my hand to squeeze it comfortingly. When I look up at him, his eyes are shiny with tears too.

"...the family asked that we make a special mention of the students who got together and raised money for Tracey, so we did. Page 84 of your yearbook is a page just for Tracey." She raises her voice over the sudden rustle as we all open our yearbooks to see the big page full of pictures of Tracey laughing and smiling.

Mrs. Sparks is still talking, but for once I'm not paying attention. At the bottom of the page, in a little box, it says, "Thank you to the Secret Sisters Club for bringing the light of friendship into a dark time."

Tears run down my cheeks and I look up at my friends. They are crying, too, and we all hug for what seems like a long time.

"All right," Mrs. Sparks says, rubbing a few tears from her own eyes. "Now it's time for report cards."

As all the report cards are passed out, I feel another jolt of nerves. I'm not sure why, but it almost feels like something bad is going to happen. I sit with my hands balled up into fists in my lap.

Curtis looks at me curiously, then takes one of my hands in his. "Are you okay?" he asks, his hazel eyes worried.

I try for a small smile, but it looks so fake he can tell there's something wrong. Barbara and Kendall get back with their report cards then, so I'm saved from having to explain something I'm not sure of myself.

"Look!" Barbara says, pushing her report card into my face. "I got a C in math! I was sure I would fail it and have to go to summer school. Thank you so much for tutoring me, Destiny."

"I got all B's," Kendall says with a satisfied smile. "That's pretty good. Yeah, thanks Destiny."

I shrug, my face getting warm even though I'm happy. "You two helped me with my poetry reading, so I was glad to help with math."

Curtis raises his eyebrows. "Maybe you can help me with math when I get back from basketball camp," he says with a smile. "I don't know what my grade is, but I had a lot of trouble with it this year."

Before I have a chance to do more than nod, Mrs. Sparks calls my name. As I walk up to get my report card, she beams at me. "Destiny is our only student this year to receive a straight-A honor roll for the entire year. We're all very proud of her." She claps and all the parents and students join in the applause. I feel like I'm getting a medal when Mrs. Sparks hands me the report card.

I turn to go sit with my friends again, but I see Mrs. Grant, the math teacher, waving me closer. She never wants to talk to anyone, so at first I'm surprised. When I get to her, she smiles. She doesn't smile a lot, but when she does it makes her dark olive skin look like it's glowing. "Congratulations on your grades, Destiny. Your parents must be very proud."

I look at Momma and she's dabbing her eyes with a handkerchief. "I think so," I tell her. When Mrs. Grant raises one eyebrow, I hurry to add, "They think education is really important, so yeah I'm sure they are."

"Well," Mrs. Grant says, smoothing her blouse, "Mr. Gabriel and I have been talking about you."

"You have?" I look at Mr. Gabriel, sitting in the row of chairs behind the podium, his bald head shiny under the gym lights. Why would they talk about me? I didn't do anything wrong.

Mrs. Grant seems to see that I'm worried. "Good things, Destiny," she assures me. "I'd like you to meet me after the ceremony to talk about your future."

"Okay," I say and Mrs. Grant nods before turning her attention back to what Mrs. Sparks is saying. I return to my seat quietly, not sure what to think.

"Now, it's time for the eighth grader of the year award," Mrs. Sparks says as I settle into my spot between Barbara and Curtis. "This is our highest honor, given to the student who inspires and motivates all of us, both students and teachers, to be a better person..."

She's still talking about the award, but I keep thinking about Mrs. Grant. I've always liked her, but she never wants to talk to any of the kids unless she has to, and usually she frowns a lot. She says it's something good, but I'm still nervous.

"This is a student from whom we expect great things in the coming years, so it is both an honor and a privilege…," Mrs. Sparks continues.

I fidget in my seat. What if she thinks I need summer school? I like to learn, but there's nothing in the classes I took this year that I need work on.

"Linelle Destiny Sycamores!" Mrs. Sparks says loudly and I jump. What just happened?

Chapter Nine
Award

Kendall and Barbara fly out of their seats, jumping up and down and screaming. As they pull me out of my seat, Curtis grins at me. Did I just win eighth grader of the year?

The whole Secret Sisters Club is standing and clapping for me, cheering me on as I slowly walk toward the podium. I look back at them as I walk, wondering if there's been some kind of mistake. As I look through the crowd of cheering friends, I see one person who doesn't look happy at all. Haley is glaring at me, her arms crossed tight over her chest. A chill runs up my spine as I see her, but Kendall waves me forward and the warm feeling from having so many good friends covers up any nervousness about Haley.

Mrs. Sparks calls Momma up as I get to the podium and I feel like I'm drifting through a great dream. Momma hugs me tight, her eyes filled with tears.

"I'm so proud of you, Destiny. I'm gonna have to tell your Aunt Shirley how special my little girl is and what a big difference she made in her school."

She lets me go and I can't help but feel pride like a huge balloon blowing up in my chest. Let Aunt Shirley gossip about that! It's the most perfect day I can imagine.

"I hope you're happy!" A shrill shriek cuts through the air and a sudden silence follows it as we all look toward Haley. She's standing right in front of the podium, her hands clenched into fists at her sides. Her caramel-colored face is such a deep shade of red I'm worried she will pass out. All my nerves and bad feelings from earlier come zinging back to life, zapping my floaty dreamland and popping the big bubble of happiness in my chest.

It's so terribly quiet. "W-w-w...," I begin, then look at Kendall and Barbara, reminding myself how they taught me to stop stuttering. I relax my throat, then try again. "What's the matter, Haley?"

"I'll tell you w-w-w-what's the matter," she mocks me, her face all wrinkled and ugly in a sneer. "You cheated to get good grades, you stole my boyfriend, and you lied to get my father kicked out of the ceremony. Then you stole my award!"

I'm so shocked that I can't think of anything to say, so I just stare at her. So does everyone else.

"I've worked all year," she shouts, then jabs a finger at me, "in your stupid sisters club, and you never did anything for the club. You didn't even lead it, even though you were president! But even that's not enough. You went and started gossiping about me to Curtis, so he would break up with me and date you."

"Hey!" Kendall shouts, her dark eyebrows scrunching together in anger. "We all voted her in and it's not her fault that your boyfriend dumped you."

Haley ignores her, keeping her eyes on me. I've never seen her like this before. It scares me a little. "Tell everyone how you lied, how you cheated, how you took everything that was mine!"

"Haley...," I start to say, but Momma's hand on my shoulder makes me quiet down.

"You don't have to listen to her, baby," Momma tells me, pulling me close and hugging me. "It's alright, don't cry."

I didn't even realize I was crying, but when I reach up to touch my face, I feel more hot tears running over my fingers. I hold back a sob, sniffling as Momma looks up at Haley.

"Shame on you," she says quietly, but somehow her words seem to fill the room. "I've seen how hard Destiny works, every night she's up late studying, working on her club, and helping other people. Someone who wants to take away credit from a person who does all that doesn't deserve an award."

Haley is looking around at everyone, too, her face getting even redder as she realizes no one agrees with her. "Fine!" she snaps, spinning on her heel and stomping out. "I'll make my own club and everyone will want to join! Everyone can gossip and it'll be for boys and girls! Everyone will quit your stupid club and join mine!" She slams the door of the gym behind her and it seems to break the spell.

Everyone starts fidgeting and muttering, their eyes still wide with shock.

I look at Momma and she has more love for me in her eyes than I've ever seen. When I look around at everyone, they're all nodding in agreement. "I didn't know you noticed," I tell her and she smiles.

"I notice more than you think, honey."

As we all walk out of the gym together, Curtis puts his arm around my shoulders and squeezes tight. It makes the butterflies in my stomach jump a little when he does that, but I like the feel of his arm around my shoulders. I pretend not to notice it and hope Momma won't tell Aunt Shirley about my new boyfriend. She probably will, though. "Don't worry about your club," Curtis says. "I'm sure that everyone will stay with you."

Kendall looks uncomfortable. "I don't know. A lot of the girls were upset that we couldn't have boys in the club. They might join Haley's club just for that."

Barbara shrugs. "I was talking to a few people and it might not matter anyway, at least for the summer."

I look over at her, raising one eyebrow. "What do you mean?"

"So many people are going on summer trips and having to go to summer school or moving away. It's going to be hard to keep the club together over the summer."

"How many people?" I ask and Barbara starts naming people. As the list grows, I put my hands on my hips. "That's almost the whole club!"

Kendall snorts. "Even most of Haley's group are going to be gone. She's going to have a hard time making a new club with herself and one other person."

I nod, but I'm not worried about Haley's new club. Not as much as I'm worried about losing our club over the summer. "What are we gonna do?" I whine, my voice getting higher.

"You can add boys to your club," Curtis jokes. "It could be the Secret Not-quite-sisters Club."

I laugh. "Or the Secret Not-all-of-us-are-sisters Club." We all laugh, but afterward we look at each other sadly.

"Well, you didn't have much money left for more meetings or club birthday parties anyway," Kendall tells me. "Those last four birthday parties and the donation to Tracey brought our treasury way down."

I sigh. We had been renting a meeting room at the public library for only five dollars, but even that was too expensive if the treasury was empty. "I just wanted a club where everyone could be together and help each other," I say and all three of them nod.

"You did help people," Barbara tells me, gently. "Just because we might not be in a club over the summer doesn't mean we didn't have a great club during the school year."

Kendall nods. "I don't know if I would have made it through the year without the club. All the stuff at my house, with the guy selling and us moving..." Her voice trails off as two splotches of pink show up on her golden cheeks. "The Secret Sisters Club really helped me through and I don't think I'm the only one."

"I'm gonna miss the newspaper," I say. We had been publishing a newspaper every month. It was always a fun way to keep up with school events.

"Me too," Kendall says. "Maybe I'll start up a newspaper at my new school."

"I'll miss the club birthday parties," Barbara pipes up. "I really liked setting up parties for everyone and my party was so much fun. I wasn't even going to get a birthday party with all my friends, so I'm glad the club had one."

"So what are you going to do?" Curtis asks, hugging my shoulder a little. I lean against him a bit, while I think. The other three stand still and watch me.

"Maybe we should let the club rest a little bit over the summer," I tell them, finally. I hate saying it, but I can't think of anything else to do. "Then we can try to get the club back together next year."

"What are you gonna do instead?" Barbara asks. "You're the only one of us who doesn't have something to do over the summer."

I shrug. "Not sure. I want to do something good for people," I say, then think for a moment. "I want to deserve that eighth grader of the year award."

Kendall snorts. "You deserve it more than any of us. Don't let Haley make you think that you don't."

I smile at Kendall, then sigh. "I'm not sure what to do about the award, really."

"Actually, I think I might be able to answer that question, Destiny," Mrs. Grant says from behind us.

Chapter Ten
Epilogue

I completely forgot that Mrs. Grant wanted to talk to me. I say a quick goodbye to all my friends and Mrs. Grant and I hurry back in to find my Momma. She is talking to a group of parents and she looks worried even though Mrs. Grant assures her that everything is fine. I feel a lot better that I'm not the only one who gets nervous about a talk with Mrs. Grant.

We choose a table and Mrs. Grant settles herself into a chair carefully. The way her hands flutter as she thinks about what to say seems odd. It's almost like she's nervous and I've never seen Mrs. Grant nervous before. I give her my most encouraging smile and she smiles back thinly in return.

"I spoke with Mr. Gabriel earlier today," she says, glancing between me and my mother with a hawk like stare. "You are an exceptional student, Destiny, and we believe that you can achieve great things." She pauses, staring me in the eyes.

I can feel my cheeks getting hot as I blush, even though she didn't say it like it was a compliment. "Thank you," I reply.

Mrs. Grant shakes her head. "But you have to do something with all that potential. Your club and tutoring your friends in math are a great start." When my eyes fly wide open, she raises a hand. "Yes, I've known all about the extra help you have given Barbara and Kendall. They started solving their math problems exactly like you do and I'm not sure they would have gotten through it if you hadn't helped them."

Momma is looking back and forth between us with interest, her chin propped up in her hand. "They helped me recite my poetry in front of the class," I say and Mrs. Grant nods.

Then, Mrs. Grant clears her throat. "But Destiny, you've got to get your head right. The more you concentrate on boys and clubs, the more opportunities will pass you by." She gives me another hawk stare and I fidget nervously. "You have a chance right now to advance to tenth grade, if you can prove that you are able to handle the subject matter. You would pass by the other students in your class and graduate high school a year early."

I sit back in my chair, stunned. I can skip a grade? That must be why she had to talk to Mr. Gabriel. Maybe they wanted to talk to Momma and me together, because she won't want me to. I sneak a peek over at her and she is looking back at me, her eyes sparkling.

"This is your choice," Momma tells me. "I won't make it for you."

I look down at the tabletop. It's an exciting idea, but do I want to do this?

Mrs. Grant seems to know what I'm thinking. "You will have to leave your friends behind to do this and it will take a lot of work to make sure you keep up with your new classmates. I'd recommend you come and take some time at the summer school."

When I look at her, confused, she smiles.

"Not all summer school classes are for people who failed. You can go into some of the ninth grade level classes and listen in. Not as a student, but as a teacher's assistant. You could also hold tutoring sessions with some of the other students, if you wanted. That way you can learn the new material and practice your teaching skills at the same time. You would be able to charge for your time, so you could earn a little money on the side."

My head is spinning. "Like a summer job?" I ask.

Mrs. Grant nods. "You'd have to be there on time every day and be willing to help me grade papers and print out lesson plans. You would also get your own book. You can talk to the other teachers as well, but I know a few of them would love if you helped out in their classes as well." She pauses. "This isn't an easy thing, Destiny. If you don't want to leave your friends or you find out over the summer that you aren't ready to move up to the next class, it's alright."

"I'll have to think about it," I say, "but I think I'd like to try helping out at summer school."

"Excellent," Mrs. Grant says, then stands up. As we all come to our feet together, she smiles at me, the hawk like stare evaporating in a happy smile. "Your life is just beginning, Destiny. Take hold of it and what happens after that will make you happier than you ever could have imagined."

She walks away, and as I listen to the click of her heels on the floor of the gym, I feel like my story is only beginning.

About the Author

Alicia Linelle Holland was born and raised in Many, Louisiana and got her middle name after her mother, Vera Linelle. When Alicia was in middle school, she started the Secret Sister Club that you read about in the Linelle Destiny Book Series. Alicia Holland has been working towards bringing back the Secret Sister Club as she embarks upon quite an interesting life and spiritual journey. At age 26, she earned her Doctorate in Education so that she can be in a position to help others believe in themselves and go far. At age 31, Dr. Alicia Holland opened a Not for Profit, Alise Spiritual Healing & Wellness Center and was officially ordained as a Minister. As a Transformational Life Coach, Professor, Author, Speaker, and Minister, Dr. Holland travels the World sharing her message: "You are Loved, You are Valued, and You are Competent.

Dr. Alicia Holland has two beautiful daughters, ages 7 and 9, who travels the World with her and are active participants in the Secret Sister Club Mentoring Program. She and her family resides in Austin, Texas and are currently looking for a new puppy.

Dr. Holland is available for speaking engagements and can be reached at support@thesecretsistersclub.com or support@iglobaleducation.com.

www.ingramcontent.com/pod-product-compliance
Lightning Source LLC
Chambersburg PA
CBHW070535130626
46555CB00003B/1430